GORMY RUCKLES
MONSTER MISCHIEF

GUY BASS
Illustrations by Ross Collins

SCHOLASTIC

Look out for other monster adventures:

Meet the Ruckles

(and then run away!)

Gormy Ruckles, the monster boy, was very
small, very blue and very hairy. He had a
long tail and just one quite good fang.
Gormy lived at No.1 Peatree Hill with his
mother, Mogra the Horrid, and his father,
Grumbor the Grim. If you ever find
yourself passing by Peatree Hill, do feel
free to pop in.

I'm sure they'll have you for dinner!

To Ian
The master of monsters

First published in the UK in 2008 by Scholastic Children's Books
An imprint of Scholastic Ltd
Euston House, 24 Eversholt Street
London, NW1 1DB, UK
Registered office: Westfield Road, Southam, Warwickshire, CV47 0RA
SCHOLASTIC and associated logos are trademarks and/or registered
trademarks of Scholastic Inc.

ISBN 978 1 407 10460 7

A CIP catalogue record for this book
is available from the British Library

Printed in the UK by CPI Bookmarque, Croydon
Papers used by Scholastic Children's Books are made from
wood grown in sustainable forests.

5 7 9 10 8 6 4

This is a work of fiction. Names, characters, places, incidents and
dialogues are products of the author's imagination or are used fictitiously.
Any resemblance to actual people, living or dead, events or locales
is entirely coincidental.

www.scholastic.co.uk/zone

OnE

How to Throw rocks and Influence People

Gormy sat at the breakfast table, eating his bowl of hamsters so quickly that he started to cough up hairballs.

"Gormy Ruckles, what have I told you about chewing your food? Do you want to give yourself gut-ache?" asked Gormy's mother. Gormy decided it was one of those questions he didn't really have to answer. Why would anyone *want* to give themselves gut-ache? Apart from the Witch of Goggan Moor, who only ate angry wasps.

"Can I get down from the table?" asked Gormy, although with his mouth full it sounded like, "Cud I geddum bubba day-bull?". Gormy's mother understood him perfectly. After all, it's rude *not* to talk with your mouth full at a monster's table.

"You *may* not go anywhere until you've finished your breakfast," she said. Gormy's mother was a large, pink monster, and was at least forty-eight times more monstrous than any mother you've ever met. She was as big as two hippos glued together and had more hair than all three finalists in last year's Hideously Hairy Monster contest.

Who cares about breakfast on a day like this? thought Gormy. Today was more monstrously exciting than the first Monstrously Exciting Day – the day when the first monster, Mon the Monstrous, scared his first woolly mammoth!

Today was ROCK THROWING DAY!

Gormy had never had a lesson in throwing before. The ability to throw a really big rock (or tree or horse or cow) was the measure of a truly monstrous monster. As Gormy's father, Grumbor, always said, "A hoomum will be twice as scared of a monster who can throw than one who can't." Grumbor was especially good at throwing things. He had won the silver medal at the Monster's Third National Throwing, Hurling and Lobbing tournament, and had twice broken the world record for long-distance Sheep Tossing.

Gormy had already written the lesson number in his **How to be a Better Monster** book. He opened the book and stared gleefully at the page.

"*Please* may I please get down from the table?" he begged, before swallowing the last of his hamsters.

Gormy's mother looked at him sternly.

"Where are your manners today, Gormy?" she asked.

"Oh sorry, Mum," said Gormy, then let out an almighty

BUUURRRP!

"That's better," said Gormy's mother. "Now run along."

TWO

Do Not Throw

Gormy scampered out of the kitchen door as fast as his hairy, blue legs could carry him. He had made it halfway down the garden when he heard a tiny, gruff voice.

"Where are you off to then?"

"Mike!" said Gormy.

Perched on a monster-sized plant pot

was his only real friend, Mike the Scuttybug. Mike looked how a beetle would look in a nightmare about ugly, monstrous beetles. He was greasy, green and smelled faintly of his favourite food – poo.

"Thinking of doing a spot of throwing, are we?" Mike asked. "I've been watching your dad lobbing rocks all morning."

"I'm going to be the best thrower ever! Hop on, quick," said Gormy, offering Mike a furry, blue paw.

Mike scuttied on to Gormy's arm and they made their way to the bottom of the garden. It wasn't long before they spotted Gormy's father.

Grumbor Ruckles was a huge, dark blue monster, with tusks as big as branches. He had more monstrousness per square inch than any other monster in the valley. He was standing by the thick wall of trees that surrounded the house, and throwing large rocks right over it.

"Dad!" cried Gormy excitedly. Grumbor turned just as he was about to throw. The rock flew out of his hand towards Gormy.

"Eek!"

squeaked
Gormy and
Mike together,
before jumping out of
the way of the boulder. It

whooshed past Gormy's head and crashed on to the lawn.

"You know better than to sneak up on a monster when he's throwing things," grumbled Grumbor as he lumbered towards Gormy. "The key to monstering is keeping your head while all about you are having theirs knocked off. Are you all right?"

"Yeah, great!" said Gormy. Now he was even *more* excited about his lesson. Having things thrown at you was nearly as monstrous as throwing them! He stared at the rock next to him. "Can I throw it? Can I?" he asked.

"Let's start with something a little smaller," said Grumbor, before loping back down the garden. Gormy and Mike followed him to a huge pile of rocks of various sizes and shapes. There must have been a hundred of them! Maybe even a hundred and two! (Monsters can count piles of things very quickly.) Grumbor searched through the rocks until. . .

"A-ha! This one should do for starters. Hold out your hand."

Gormy's father didn't seem to be holding anything at all. He just had his finger and thumb pressed carefully together. He reached over to Gormy, and opened his fingers. The smallest rock in the world plopped into Gormy's hand.

"It's tiny. . ." said Gormy. "Can't I throw something bigger?"

"Don't try to stomp before you can walk," said Grumbor. "Now then, let's see you throw that rock over the trees."

Gormy looked down at the pebble his father had given him, and shrugged. He

reached his arm all
the way back, and
threw!

plud

The rock landed at
the edge of the trees,
only a few paces from
where Gormy
and his father
were standing.

"Nice try," said Mike, sort of
encouragingly.

"Still too big, need something smaller,"
Grumbor mumbled to himself. Of course,
as a monster, even his quietest mumble was
really quite easy to hear. Gormy's pointy
blue ears drooped with disappointment as
Grumbor pulled out an even tinier pebble

11

from the pile.

"Try imagining you're aiming at something," said Grumbor. "Pretend that on the other side of those trees is a herd of really evil goats. Or a big hoomum village! Yes, pretend that when you throw your rock, it lands on a nice, new hoomum house."

Gormy imagined a lovely hoomum house, built out of the finest wood and thatch. He imagined several hoomums standing next to it and saying things like "This is the nicest house we've ever built!" and "I do hope nothing bad happens to it!"

"SMASH!" said Gormy with glee. He gripped the rock tightly between his paws and threw the rock as hard as he could.

CluD

It bounced off the trunk of a tree and

rolled back into the garden. Gormy deflated like a balloon. He looked up at his father, but Grumbor simply shook his head a little.

"Not ready. . ." he mumbled.

"I am ready, I am!" cried Gormy in desperation. "I can throw the biggest rock in the garden! I can. . ."

It was then Gormy spotted it. A large, grey rock, set apart from the pile. It was unremarkable except for one thing. Carved into the face of the rock were three words:

"What about that one?" said Gormy.

Gormy's father laughed so loudly that all the birds in the trees flew off in fright, and kept flying until they were quite lost and had to make new homes in new trees far, far away.

"That rock's for monsters, not monster *boys*," said Grumbor. "That's the DO NOT THROW rock. It's the most *unthrowable*

rock in world. For centuries, monsters came to Peatree Hill to try and throw this rock. It was the greatest challenge any monster could face. One after the other they came, so that they might be declared Most Monstrous Monster (Probably in the World) Ever. Many monsters have tried to throw it. None have succeeded. Most have actually exploded."

"Explo . . . plo . . . ploded?" said Gormy, his blue lips quivering.

"Did I not mention that before? Oh yes, Rock-throwing is a very explosion-heavy pastime. It's one of the few things that can make a monster pop without the slightest warning. Even an expert rock-thrower must be on his guard. A careless lift here, a sloppy lob there, and **boom!** No more monster."

"Can . . . can *you* throw the DO NOT THROW rock?" stuttered Gormy.

"What, and risk exploding all over the flower beds? Your mother would kill me! No, I've realized this rock simply *cannot* be thrown. That's why I carved DO NOT THROW on to its face.

"I bet *I* can throw it!" said Gormy confidently. This time Grumbor did not laugh.

"I said *no*," he said sternly. "It's too dangerous, and you're much too young to be exploding. That rock *cannot* be thrown. And unless you want to be sent to your room for a hundred years, you'll leave it well alone. Do I make myself clear?"

"Yes, Dad," said Gormy quietly.

"We'll come back to throwing when you're ready, when you're older. Maybe next year," said Grumbor. "Now go and help your mother with the housework."

Next year? Gormy thought. *Housework?*

This was turning out to be the worst day *ever*.

Three

Throwing the Unthrowable

That night, Gormy lay awake in bed. An idea was forming in his brain. The idea had just started turning into a plan when Mike scuttied in through his window.

"Still thinking about the DO NOT THROW rock?" said Mike.

"How did you know?" asked Gormy.

"Oh, I know that *thinking-about-doing-something-you-shouldn't-think-about-doing* look. You get it almost every day."

"Well, *this* time it'll be worth it," said Gormy.

Gormy waited until his parents had gone to sleep, then he and Mike sneaked downstairs. They crept out of the back door and down the garden. There, in the moonlight, was the DO NOT THROW rock.

"I don't know about this, Gormy," said Mike. "You don't want to explode. Or even worse, get in trouble with your dad."

But Gormy wasn't listening. He grasped the rock at the base with both paws. It was five times bigger than he was and eleventeen times as heavy. Gormy held his breath and lifted with all his might. His blue face went purple and his fur stood on end. His whole body began to shake, and steam shot out of his ears. A sound came from his nose which sounded exactly like fifty pigs falling off a cliff. He started sweating green smoke, then made this noise, which was the very first noise of its kind:

"GaNNNaBhUrNababaF eeeTPuPTooOOOoGN!"

"Blimey!" said Mike. "You're doing it!"

As slowly as the workings of a sheep's brain, Gormy lifted the unthrowable rock above his head. By now, Gormy was fairly

convinced that he was going to explode any
second. But what a way to go! He
summoned every last ounce of his strength,
and threw!

Thod

"Blimey! you did it!" said Mike.

"I did it!" repeated Gormy. A new-found
sense of monstrousness filled him to the
brim. He hadn't thrown the rock very far,
but he hadn't exploded either! He grabbed
Mike and hugged him in delight. He didn't
even mind how slimy and pooey Mike was!
It was a few moments later that he noticed
a small, dark blob where the DO NOT
THROW rock used to stand. It was very
much like any other small, dark blob, and
really not much to look at.

That is, until it started to move.

Four

The Thing Under the Rock

Gormy and Mike stared as the dark blob began to uncurl. A long spindly arm appeared, then another! Shortly after that a leg appeared. The shape unfolded and unfurled until, finally, it had a head, two arms and two legs. It was an odd-looking something-or-other, even by monstrous

standards. It was a little
smaller than Gormy,
with a round body and
long, thin limbs. Its
skin was smooth and
shiny and it had a
round head, and
gleaming, beady eyes.

"What is it?"
whispered Gormy.

"Dunno," replied Mike.

"Bless my bones! What a relief!
I was mashed under there
like some tenderized beef.
My legs are all crunchy,
my arms are all dangled!
And look here at this,
my nose has been mangled!"

The something-or-other rubbed its nose back into shape, before fixing its gaze on a puzzled Gormy.

"Um, hello," said Gormy. "My name's Gormy Ru—"

"The question to ask is:
what is my name?
One day to the next, it is never the same!
In the east, I'm Old Nucksy,
or 'Nucks' if you wish,
but west of the glen
I'm the Black Stony Fish.
Where there's sea and there's sand,
call me Tricksy-to-Tell.
But I'll give you a secret,
since you've treated me well."

"What's he on about?" asked Mike.

"What secret?" said Gormy, trying to keep up. The something-or-other jumped up and down in excitement.

"My secret name!
It's the point of this rhyme,
so keep it remembered
and keep it in mind!
For if you forget it,
I'll never be seen,
but you'll know I'm around
by the trouble there's been."

"Blimey, he goes on a bit, doesn't he?" said Mike.

"So without more ado
(and so you don't make a fuss)

I present you my name,
it's THE IKUM FLOOKUS!"

Then for no reason at all, the
something-or-other started to giggle. It
giggled and giggled and giggled, and as it
giggled, it started to fade. Within
moments, it had vanished into thin air!

"That's a nice trick," said Mike. "He
could use that at parties."

"What was that all about?" said
Gormy.

"Beats me," said Mike. "I tell you what
though – throwing that unthrowable rock
makes you at least twice as monstrous as
any monster I've ever seen!"

Gormy swelled with pride. Even though
he could never tell his father that he'd
disobeyed him (for fear of being sent to his

room *for ever*) he was delighted to be the Most Monstrous Monster (Probably in the World) Ever!

Gormy said goodnight to Mike and crept back into the house. It wasn't until he was climbing into bed that he heard something behind him. He turned around to see his bedroom door swinging on its hinges, but there was nothing there.

Just the faint sound of giggling. . .

Five

Morning Mischief

When Gormy awoke the next day, he had all but forgotten about the giggling something-or-other. Anyway, he was so excited about how monstrous he had become that nothing else seemed to matter.

Gormy trekked excitedly across the bathroom (which, like all the rooms in the house, was monstrously big) and began the long climb up to the sink. At the top he began his usual routine of fur washing and fang brushing. Now you might think that being clean and being monstrous are two very different things, but as Gormy's father always said, "The key to monstering is to know *why* you're monstrous. If you smell bad, how will you know whether it is you, or your smell, that is terrifying?"

Gormy had just squeezed some fangpaste on to his brush when he heard a giggling sound behind him. He looked round just in time to see the door open and close all on its own! He would have thought more about it, but as he put the fangbrush into his mouth. . .

"Bleurgh!"

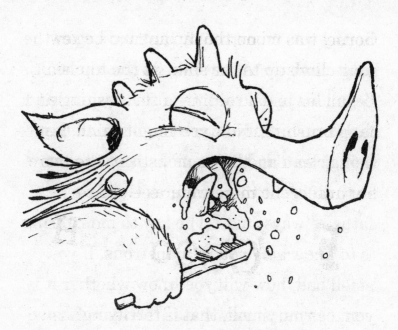

said Gormy. It wasn't fangpaste at all! Fangpaste (as anyone with a passing knowledge of monsters will tell you) is black with green stripes and tastes like sweaty armpits. This was all blue and minty-tasting! It was the most horrible thing Gormy had ever tasted, and he had to try very hard not to be sick. In an attempt to wash away the freakishly fresh taste,

Gormy turned on the tap and took a few gulps of water. After spitting into the sink, he turned off the tap. Or at least, he tried to. He turned and turned and turned, but the tap wouldn't turn off. In fact, the more he turned, the more water seemed to

FoOOoooooSH

out. Gormy turned and turned and turned until. . . **tunk!**

The tap came off in his hands!

Gormy hung on to what was left of the tap as the water flowed more and more quickly into the sink. It poured over the rim and

KoSOOOShed

on to the floor.

It'll fill the whole bathroom! thought Gormy. He decided this was one of those extremely rare moments when he really should get his parents. He tried scrambling down from the sink but the water carried him over the edge. He landed on the floor with a **SPOSH!** By now the water was spilling over the sink like an enormous waterfall. It began to fill the bathroom. Within moments the water rose from Gormy's knees to his chin. He banged on the door.

"Mum! Dad!" he cried. It was the last thing he said before the water lifted him off his feet. He was flung, weightless, around the room. Soon the whole room would be filled and he would be under water! Gormy was just starting to get a bit worried when he spotted the door handle. There was only one thing for it – Gormy took a deep breath into all of his four lungs (and a small one into his spare lung) and dived under. He swam as hard as he could towards the handle. He had to dodge a bar of soap and his father's favourite rubber duck, but before long he made it! He grabbed the handle and turned with all his might.

After a few (very long) seconds, Gormy felt the giant bathroom handle turn. The door swung open with an almighty

SPOOOOOOOOSSSSH!

The great tidal wave of water cascaded out of the bathroom and down the stairs! Gormy was carried helplessly down the

bump

poosh

Slish

Slish

bump

bu-dump

ga-damp

stairs (along with most of the contents of the bathroom!) and all the way to the bottom, through the hall and into the kitchen, before skidding to a halt at his mother's feet.

"Gormy Ruckles, what on Peatree Hill have you done?"

"N-not me!" gasped Gormy, dragging himself to his feet. "The t-tap. . ."

"Are you trying to drown us all?" asked

Gormy's mother. Gormy was about to protest his innocence when he heard *that* sound again. That *giggling* sound. He looked around to see the kitchen door open and swing shut . . . all on its own!

"Did you see that?" he said.

"Don't interrupt!" screeched Gormy's mother. "Honestly, Gormy, sometimes I wonder what goes on in that little blue head of yours. Look at this mess! Well, if you've time enough to get into mischief, you've time enough to clean all this up."

"But it wasn't—" began Gormy.

"And when you're finished with that, you can do the washing up!" continued his mother.

"And when you're done with *that* you can help me paint the shed," said Grumbor, strolling into the hall. "Looks like you've got a busy day ahead. . ."

"But . . . but. . ." Gormy began.

"But me no buts, I'll have no buts butted about," said Gormy's mother. "I need everything to be perfect tonight. We have the Boggles family coming for dinner."

Not the Boggles! Anyone but the Boggles! thought Gormy.

The Boggles were a family of monsters from the next valley. Mrs Boggles was big and boring and *never* stopped talking. She especially liked to talk about her son, Poggy. Poggy Boggles thought he was the most monstrous monster boy in the whole world. He had a proper roar, could scare six different types of livestock and had two, yes two, long, sharp fangs. Even if Poggy had been the nicest monster-boy in the valley (which he wasn't) Gormy would have disliked him intensely.

"Smelly-face Poggy," mumbled Gormy, even though he knew Poggy's face didn't smell of anything much.

"So we'll have none of this nonsense," said Gormy's mother. "I want you on your best behaviour. If in doubt, just copy Poggy Boggles. I *don't* want you showing me up, not when Poggy is so *monstrously* well behaved. You see, he knows the difference between being monstrous and just being mischievous. So? What do you want? Do you want to be monstrous . . . or mischievous?"

"Monstrous," replied Gormy quietly. In fact, he had never felt *less* monstrous in his whole life.

Six

Seventy-seven Saucepans

Gormy had been washing up monstrously dirty saucepans for most of the day. As he polished the seventy-seventh of them to a impressive sheen, he felt rather proud of himself. Each pan gleamed only slightly less brightly than Vongur the Blaze, whose head was an actual sun. Gormy stepped back to admire his gloriously horrible reflection in one of the pans. He was baring his one quite good fang when (for the third time that morning) he heard the strange giggling sound. He spun around to see the kitchen door swing on its hinges.

There it is again! he thought. *The giggling something-or-other from last night! What was it called? The Ookum Fleekus? No, that's not it. . .* Gormy put the giggling something-or-other's name to the back of his mind for the moment. He pinned back his pointy, blue ears, and followed the giggling sound upstairs.

"I can hear you!" said Gormy. He searched his room, his parents' bedroom, the spare room and even the room of doom and gloom (which, it turned

out, was just a big cupboard) but there was
no sign of anyone. *Where can it be?* thought
Gormy. He was about to give up when he
heard a sound so deafening that the whole
of Peatree Hill jumped into the air.

Goooorrrrmmmy!!!

Gormy raced downstairs to the kitchen!
He was met at the door by his mother,
looking even angrier than the time he'd
accidentally eaten her pet squirrel.

"What in the name of the Seven Signs of
Monstering do you call this?"

Gormy peered around the kitchen door.
He immediately wondered how long he'd
been upstairs. The saucepans were covered
in paint! All seventy-seven had been
daubed, splashed and dunked in a bright
combination of blues, pinks and yellows

(the colours of a monstrous shed!). Not
only that, but the whole kitchen was

covered. The walls dripped with paint,
plipping and plopping into bright pools on
the floor. Even the air was thick with a
painty fog, which settled like multicoloured
dew on Gormy's fur.

"I . . . I didn't . . . I . . . I cleaned. . ." began Gormy, his eyes wide with disbelief.

"You call this CLEANING?" bellowed Gormy's mother, her words sparking like lightning in the air. "Is this your idea of a joke? Well, I'll tell you what, there's a time and a place for jokes, and it's at four-fourteen on the fifth of Febtember at the Festival of Foolery and Flim-Flam! It's NOT when we're about to have the Boggles over for dinner! What were you thinking?"

"But it wasn't me! I polished—" began Gormy.

"This is exactly the sort of behaviour I was talking about!" interrupted Gormy's mother. "I can't imagine Poggy making mischief, can you? I can't imagine Mr and Mrs Boggles having to tell Poggy not to splash paint all over the kitchen!"

By now, Gormy's mother was shouting so loudly that Gormy almost didn't hear the sound of giggling.

I knew it! thought Gormy. *It's the Ookum Fleekus . . . the giggling something-or-other! It's trying to get me into trouble!* He was about to tell his mum all about the DO NOT THROW rock and the giggling something-or-other when he heard his father's voice.

"Who's used up all my paint?" said Grumbor, coming into the kitchen from the garden. He was holding the one remaining tin of bluey-pinky-yellow paint.

"Um . . . it was . . . the . . . uh. . . ." Gormy stuttered. He knew he couldn't tell his father about the giggling something-or-other without revealing where it had come from, and that would mean being sent to his room for a hundred years. That was a long time – even for a monster. He bit his lip and said nothing.

"At least have the good manners to admit to what you've done! Go to your room!" screamed Gormy's mother, the hairs on the back of her neck (all three thousand and eight of them) standing angrily on end. She carried on screaming so loudly that Gormy didn't even hear the sound of giggling which followed him up the stairs. . .

Seven

A Sticky Situation

Gormy made his way to his room and angrily kicked open the door. He lazily pushed the door closed. His hand immediately stuck to it. He tried to pull it away, but it was glued fast! Gormy sighed a long sigh and slumped to the floor, his hand still thoroughly stuck.

"What's all this then?" said Mike as he scuttied in through Gormy's window.

"What does it look like? I'm *glued* to the door," said Gormy impatiently. "Do you remember that thing under the DO NOT THROW rock?"

"The Ookum Fleekus?" said Mike. "No, wait, that's not it. . ."

"Well, *whatever* its name is – it's been playing tricks on me all day, and I've been getting the blame. I know it's here somewhere because I can hear it giggling. But I just can't find it."

"Oh, I know that feeling. I spent a whole day following a nice smell of dung but never found it. I did find two twigs and a penny, but when you want dung, only dung will do," said Mike. He stroked his chin thoughtfully. "What we need is to plan out some sort of a plan. A plantastic, plantabulous plan to catch that Ookum Fleekus . . . Eekum Flaykus . . . giggling something-or-other and put it back where it came from."

"Yeah, right back under that stupid rock! Splat!"

The next moment, Gormy's mother burst into Gormy's room, slamming the door (and poor, stuck Gormy) hard into the wall.

"Gormy? I want you downstairs now!

Gormy? Where are you?" she barked.

"Here I ab, Mub," said Gormy, holding his squashed nose. He poked his head round the door.

"What are you doing behind there? Not planning any more *mischief*, I hope," said Gormy's mother. "Now, you listen carefully, Gormy Ruckles, because I'm only going to say this once. I don't know what's got into you, but this dinner party is happening in less than an hour, whether you like it or not. So I'm giving you a choice – you can behave yourself, or you can never see Poggy or any of your monster friends ever again. Do I make myself clear?"

Gormy didn't actually have any other friends, and he certainly didn't like Poggy, so this didn't seem like much of a threat. Still, he decided just to say "Yes, Mum," and leave it at that.

"Good," said Gormy's mother. "Oh, now, look at the time, the Boggles will be arriving in an hour! I have to check the horse is cooked!"

And with that, Gormy's mother tramped downstairs, talking to herself about the best sauce to serve with horse.

"Well, that's a bit of bad timing," said Mike. "If that Ookum thingy gets up to mischief tonight, I can't see your mum being too happy."

Gormy squinted his eyes, as if thinking very hard indeed.

"'Can't see. . .' That's it! Mike, you're a genius!"

"About time somebody noticed," said Mike, who then looked a bit confused. "Eh?"

"I've got a plan," said Gormy. "We're going to make the Ookum . . . giggling something-or-other easier to see!"

Eight

Operation Catch the Giggling Something or Other
(Or: Gormy's Secret Plan)

Sorry, this chapter is secret. You don't want the *you-know-what* finding out about it, do you?

Nine

Meet the Boggles

With the plan in place (and after Mike had kindly chewed Gormy's hand free from the door), Gormy made his way downstairs and into the dining room. Laid out on the table was the most tremendously monstrous feast Gormy had ever seen. In order of tastiness, there were:

🐾 Seven sheep, raw

🐾 Six hundred and six pounds of
lightly smoked cow

🐾 One just-ripe horse, carefully stuffed
with fifteen more horses

🐾 Bat soup, made entirely of bats
who died from a thorough batting

🐾 Three well-fed donkeys

🐾 Two hundred large pebbles, to aid digestion

🐾 Various choice morsels of hoomum

Gormy jumped as the doorbell rang.
Well, roared. Monstrous doorbells roar, wail
or sneeze, depending on the season.

"Gormy, get the door!" came his
mother's cry. "I'm up to my horns in
horse!"

Gormy scrambled and leaped his way to the handle (monsters' doors are necessarily large) and opened the door. As he landed, he was met by the smug-looking face of Poggy Boggles.

"Hello, Gormy," said Poggy. He always said "Gormy" in the same way, drawn out and sneering, as if the name didn't taste nice.

Poggy was taller than Gormy, with three beady yellow eyes, two tails, and a fairly impressive covering of neat, light-green fur all over his body. Down his back an assortment of small bumps and horns made him look particularly monstrous for his age.

"Aren't you going to grow at all, Gormy? You're just as short as last time," added Poggy.

"Not like Poggy! He's already as tall as a Brog-Mangler and twice as wide," said Mrs Boggles as she swept into the house on her four stumpy legs. She was an impressively hideous monster, with short, clawed hands and a huge green mane of hair running all the way down her back. She leaned down and poked Gormy in the belly with one of her claws. "You're not getting enough protein. Our son Poggy eats a goat a day. Two if he's been out monstering!"

Poggy's been out monstering already? thought Gormy. *But he's the same age as me!*

"Don't prod the boy," said Mr Boggles. He was smaller (and quieter) than Mrs Boggles. His skin was brown and rough like bark, and he had long back legs and a tail. He looked a bit like a cross between a tree and a dinosaur. Gormy thought he was quite nice – even if he was Poggy's dad.

"Evening, Slog! Evening, Volga!" said Gormy's mother as she came into the hall. "How lovely to see you. Why, Volga, you look simply horrendous!"

"Thank you for noticing," said Mrs Boggles. "I've just had my horns done."

"Well, do take your seats at the table. Gormy, why don't you sit next to Poggy?"

Sit next to smelly-face Poggy Boggles? This day can't get any worse! thought Gormy.

But of course, it was going to get a *lot* worse. . .

Ten

Bat Soup

As the Ruckles and the Boggles sat down for dinner, Mrs Boggles immediately started talking about Poggy again.

"Poggy's quite the monster-in-the-making," she said, forcing a chunk of horse down her throat. "He can scare, stomp and spit all at the same time. It's quite unheard of for a monster boy of his age. You should see him throw a rock, there's no ear-steam at all."

Gormy longed to tell them all about the DO NOT THROW rock. He put his hand over his mouth to stop the words coming out.

"I've thrown fourteen different things," said Poggy. "I can throw a log without thinking about it. And last week, when I was out monstering all on my own, I threw a baby cow at some hoomums. It was *so* monstrous. I'm even better at throwing than Father."

"Well, I don't know about that. . ." began Mr Boggles.

"Oh hush, dear, you can barely throw a weasel with your bad back," said Mrs Boggles. "We're hoping to get Poggy a throwing scholarship at one of the better monsterversities," said Mrs Boggles.

"Can you throw, Gormy?" scoffed Poggy, nibbling on a sheep's ear.

By now Gormy was bursting to tell them how monstrous he was!

"He's not quite managed it yet, but it

won't be long," said Gormy's mother.

"It's hard to throw anything if you're really, *really* small," said Poggy.

Small? I threw the unthrowable rock! thought Gormy. He couldn't keep quiet any longer – he decided he would rather be sent to his room for a hundred years than allow Poggy to gloat for another second.

"Well, *actually,* Poggy, I threw the—" he began.

"Gormy! Fetch another bowl of bat soup," said Grumbor.

"But I was just going to say—" began Gormy.

"*Now,*" said Grumbor, not looking up.

"Maybe he's too small to carry it," said Poggy, just loudly enough for everyone to hear.

Gormy sighed, and hopped down from

the table. He made his way into the kitchen. There was no sign (or rather, sound) of the giggling something-or-other. He fetched the soup and carried it carefully (the bowl was at least three times his size) into the dining room.

"Bat soup is my absolute favourite!" said Mrs Boggles, drooling all over the table. "Honestly, you should see our Poggy catch bats of an evening; he's as fast as a dragon!"

"Bats are easy," said Poggy. "I can catch two at a time."

And with that Mrs Boggles dug her spoon into the soup.

"Ghaaaaahhh!"

she screamed as sixty enormous bats flew out! They flapped around her head like a dark cloud, getting trapped in her enormous

mane and flitting in and out of her nostrils.

"Shouldn't those bats be battered?" said Mr Boggles as he watched Mrs Boggles trying to pull them out of her nose.

"They *were* when I cooked them," said Gormy's mother, her eyes glowing a furious red. "Gormy!"

"The bats! They're flying around my brain!" screamed Mrs Boggles. By now, she had both arms all the way up her nose. Mr Boggles tried to pluck the bats out of the air with his long tongue, but he ended up wrapping it around Mrs Boggles' face.

Gormy's mother tried in vain to untangle them, all the time shouting, "GORMY! Come here this instant!"

But Gormy wasn't listening to his mother. Instead he closed his eyes, pinned back his pointy blue ears and waited for the giggling to start.

It was time to put his plan into action.

Eleven

Follow the Footprints

The giggling something-or-other's giggle was unmistakable. It was here! Amid the chaos of the bats and the entangled monsters, Gormy turned to see the kitchen door swing on its hinges.

"Mike! Now!" cried Gormy. On the other side of the kitchen door, the little scuttybug pushed hard against the last tin of bluey-pinky-yellow paint. He knocked it over and

SpLooOOOrrrp

spilled the paint all over the floor. Immediately three footprints appeared

SPLOT
SPLAT
SPLUT

in the paint! Gormy raced into the kitchen, just in time to see a trail of painty footprints leading out of the kitchen and into the hall.

"Mike! Execute Operation Catch the Ookum . . . whatever! Go to Stage Two! Stage Two!" yelled Gormy as he raced after the footprints!

"Gormy Ruckles, you get back here this INSTANT!" screamed Gormy's mother.

Gormy chased after the footprints through the hall, into the study and out into the monstering room. Two seconds later he was met by the sneering face of Poggy Boggles.

"You're in *so* much trouble, Gormy."

"Get out of the way! I've got to follow those footsteps!" said Gormy.

"It's no good making excuses, I've caught you and I'm *telling*. Run away if you like. I'll follow you and tell everyone where you are," said Poggy.

"Fine," said Gormy. "Try and keep up." Gormy pushed past Poggy, who chased after him, saying things like "I'm so telling!" and "You'll never go to monsterversity at this rate!" They raced through the hall, out of the monstering room, into the pantry, through the cellar (picking up a much-needed goat-biscuit on the way – chasing is hungry work), up the stairs, out of the bathroom, through his bedroom, past the room of doom and gloom, out of the window. . .

And on to the roof! The footprints stopped at the edge, before the long drop to the garden below.

"You're trapped, there's nowhere to run!" said Gormy. "You may as well show yourself, I know you're here!"

"Who are you talking to?" said Poggy.

"The giggling something-or-other! The Ookum Fleekus . . . oh, *whatever* it's name is!" said Gormy. Then a strange thing happened. He saw the expression on Poggy's face change. It went from its normal sour smugness, to something entirely more *horrified*.

"Not . . . you don't mean . . . not . . . the *Ikum Flookus*?" whimpered Poggy.

And with that, the Ikum Flookus appeared!

"AaaAAAaaaHH! Not again! Mother! Save me!" squealed Poggy, and ran as fast as he could in the other direction. In fact, he entirely forgot he was on the roof. He kept running into thin air and plummeted with an

AAAAAAAHHhh KLUD!

to the ground below.

"That's it!" cried Gormy. "Ikum Flookus! Your name is Ikum Flookus!"

The Ikum Flookus disappeared, then immediately reappeared. It was then that Gormy realized something very important indeed.

The name! The name made him appear and disappear!

It was too tempting not to try again.

"Ikum Flookus!" cried Gormy, and the Ikum Flookus disappeared again. "Ikum Flookus! Ikum Flookus! Ikum Flookus!" he shouted, and the Ikum Flookus disappeared and reappeared over and over.

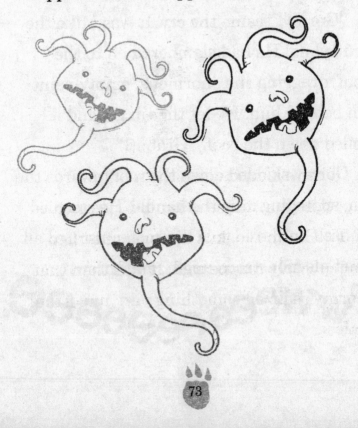

"Stop it, you gob-rot!
I'm not playing this game,
But I'll be back to torment you,
and with a new secret name!"

The Ikum Flookus leaped off the roof! It bounced like a rubber ball on the ground and started running down the garden.

"Gormy!" came the cry. It was Mike the scuttybug! He had clambered on to the roof, dragging the enormous, empty paint tin behind him. He let the tin go, and it rolled down the roof. "Grab it!"

Gormy skidded down the roof towards the tin, snatching it by the handle. He steadied himself on the edge of the roof, mustered all of his monstrous might, and threw!

Fwweeeeeeeee

The tin flew through the air! For a moment it seemed as if it would fly for ever. Then, slowly, it began to fall towards the ground. Down and down it fell, gathering speed until, **klump**

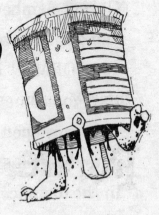

The tin landed right on top of the Ikum Flookus!

"Now *that* is throwing," said Mike.

Twelve

One More Throw Before Bedtime

Gormy clambered back into the house, and out into the garden.

"GORMY!" cried his mother. "I see you! You come here right NOW!"

Gormy sped down the garden, hotly pursued by his mother and the Boggles. In the distance, he could see the Ikum

Flookus trying to escape from under the tin, which rattled and shook. He had almost reached the tin when his mother grabbed him by the ear.

"Gormy Simpsumptitude Ruckles!" said his mother, using his incredibly embarrassing middle name (all monsters are traditionally cursed with a horrible middle name. They're considered a good way of keeping even the most monstrous monster humble). "You are in *so* much trouble! I warned you! Go to your room this instant, and don't think about coming out for a hundred, no, a *thousand* years!"

"Actually, I think he's done rather well," came a voice so thunderous that it almost started to rain. Gormy's father emerged from the shed, one of his vast arms held

77

behind his back. "You see that tin? Under that tin is an Ikum Flookus."

"What?" cried Mrs Boggles. "An *actual* Ikum Flookus?!?"

"Oh yes, an actual Ikum Flookus," repeated Grumbor with a smile. "The *same* Ikum Flookus that your son Poggy let loose in *your* house last week. The same Ikum Flookus that you begged *me* to catch because none of you could. Not even after a whole month of mischief. . ."

Poggy ran into his mother's arms. He had clearly been squashed by the fall – he was now slightly shorter than Gormy.

"Mummy! Daddy! Save me! The Ikum Flookus is after me!" he sobbed.

"No harm done," said Grumbor. He turned to Gormy. "You see, Gormy, the key to monstering is knowing when to trust in your own monstrousness. And if that means ignoring *everything* that your parents tell you, so be it. You're the first monster boy to trap an Ikum Flookus all by himself since ... well, since *I* was a monster boy."

"Oh, Grumbor, honestly!" said Gormy's mother, trying to sound disapproving. But she was so pleased that Gormy had been more monstrous than Poggy Boggles that (would you believe it?) she started to giggle.

"Shall we put things back as they should be?" Grumbor said to Gormy. He brought his mighty hand from behind his back. He was holding the DO NOT THROW rock. "I've been keeping this safe for you, Gormy. I thought you might like one more throw before bedtime."

Grumbor handed the DO NOT THROW

79

rock to Gormy, who tried not to show how
heavy it was. He summoned every last
ounce of strength, and threw!

klunch!

The rock landed on the tin, squashing it
flat and trapping the Ikum Flookus
underneath. Gormy and his father looked

at each other and smiled, while Gormy's mother shot a smug look at Mr and Mrs Boggles.

"Staying for pudding?" she asked, with a broad smile.

"Um, no, we'd better not," said Mrs Boggles. "Poggy's not very well."

"Save me, Mummy, don't let it get me. . ." squeaked Poggy, in a voice as tiny as a scuttybug's.

"Shame," said Grumbor. "See you soon. If you have any other problems with *ikum flookuses*, do let us know. I'm sure Gormy can sort it out for you."

In that moment, even Gormy started to giggle.

Thirteen

Lesson Six Hundred and Threety-three
How To Catch an Ikum Flookus

As he helped his parents clean up the
painty footprints, Gormy could hardly
believe it had all just been another lesson.
It turned out the DO NOT THROW rock
was just a rock. It wasn't unthrowable at

all. His father had just pretended it was. He knew Gormy would want to throw it and that he would accidentally release an Ikum Flookus. You see, an Ikum Flookus is just about the most mischievous, trick-playing, trouble-making creature in the world. Trapping one (even if you released one in the first place) is even more monstrous than rock-throwing.

That night, before he went to bed, Gormy opened his **How to be a Better Monster** book at a blank page. He wasn't sure what to write down. He stared out of his window, down the garden towards where the DO NOT THROW rock lay. Then he remembered what his father had said, about trusting in this own monstrousness.

"I suppose the only thing more monstrous than catching an Ikum

Flookus," said Gormy with a more-than-slightly monstrous grin, "is catching one all over again. . ."

Have you read?

Look out for more

GORMY RUCKLES

coming soon . . .

Meet Charlie – he's trouble!

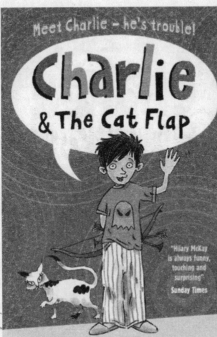

Meet Charlie – he's trouble!

Charlie
& The Cat Flap

"Hilary McKay
is always funny,
touching and
surprising"
Sunday Times

Hilary McKay

Charlie and Henry are staying the
night at Charlie's house. They've made
a deal, but the night doesn't go quite
as Charlie plans. . .

Meet Charlie – he's trouble!

Charlie's fed up with his mean family always picking on him – so he's decided to run away. That'll show them! Now they'll be sorry!

But running away means being boringly, IMPOSSIBLY quiet…